Magical Emotions

Flairs and Glairs

Publication House

"Magical Emotions"

ISBN No: " 978-93-91302-37-5"
1st Edition
Language – English and Hindi

Flairs and Glairs
Publication House
Regd. Under MSME Act.

Disclaimer

This is a work of fiction and solely represent the thoughts of the corresponding authors of the articles. Our editors have tried their best to edit the content of all the authors and check the plagiarism.

All the write-ups in this book are unique and are only published in this book.

In case any plagiarism or error is found, only the author is responsible alone, and not the publisher or the Compilers.

Cover Designing and Book Formatting
Shubham Shah and Ishani Agarwal

Co Authors

Shubham Shah (Founder Flairs and Glairs)
Ishani Agarwal (Co-Founder Flairs and Glairs)

1) Shivangi Gupta (Compiler)
2) Vasvi Ganjoos
3) Yash Sarohiwal
4) Aniket
5) Aditi Bohra
6) Dattasmita Hebburu Vishwanath
7) Swetha Reddy
8) Nidhi
9) Vaibhav Kumar Dwivedi
10) Akanksha Bawa
11) Utkarsha Phirke
12) Akash Malhotra
13) Suresh V.S
14) Jahnavi
15) Shivangi Sharma
16) Swastika Sharma
17) Kashish Jain
18) Bhavya Khanna
19) Sanjeev Kumar
20) Shri Dakshayani
21) Aakrati
22) Sandhiya Mani
23) Priyanshi Pragya
24) Susmita Negi
25) Nemi Chand Mawari
26) Shubhashree
27) Shalini
28) Roshini Agrawal

29) Manju Pb
30) Krithika Umesh
31) Kaashvi
32) Tharadara
33) Drishant Maurya
34) Mithali Singh
35) Diwan Shah
36) Nikhil K

Shubham Shah

(Founder- Flairs and Glairs)

Shubham Shah, an entrepreneur at "Flairs & Glairs" a brand with dynamics in events organizing and cultural educational pan INDIA, is a 26yrs old guy who recently has entered the digital platform of imprinting emotions. He has initiated with his own open mic platform to help budding poets and aspiring writers under his brand named as "Teekhe Zasbaaat"

He is a commerce graduate from the Bhagalpur City of Bihar. He states Writing has impersonated him since childhood and he has now been writing for over a decade!

Cooking, on the other hand, is his passion! He also mentions, trying out new things just tickles him!

When asked sir, Why SPICY EMOTIONS?

He smiled and added, "agar jasbaat teekhe na ho toh wo jasbaat kahan" Spices are all that blends! So do his words!

As a chef, he presents to you his dish! Hot and freshly served! Taste it! Feel it! Enjoy it! You can also find his writing in the Book "Teekhe Zasbaaat" and 50+ Co-authored anthologies. With his passion to explore opportunities across Platforms, he is working with keen devotion and We wish him all the very best for his future ventures.

He is Featured in the International Magazine DeMode for his upcoming solo novel.

He is Approved by Ne8x for its Lit Fest, and is a Golden Star Awards 2020 Winner.

He is a India Book of Records Holder for his Anthology Satrang, and has the Grandmaster title by Asia Book of Records, for the same.

He has also been featured in Prabhat Khabar, Dainik Jagran, and a lot of other Newspapers in Bihar for his achievements.

He has been a proud co-author to

India Book Of Records (Title- Black)

World Book Of Records (Title -15 Wonders of Poetries)

India Book Of Records (Title - Aaina)

Vajra World Records Holder (Title - Gustakhi Maaf Hai)

High Range of Records Holder (Title - Gustakhi Maaf Hai)

Indian Book of Records

(Title - Road from Worst to Best)

Share your reviews on his

INSTAGRAM
          @spicy_emotions
          @shubham4shah
Or via email on
          shubham2shah@gmail.com

To stay tuned to his work and opportunities follow his business Handles

INSTAGRAM   FACEBOOK   YOUTUBE

          @flairsandglairs
          @teekhezasbaaat

WEBSITE:
          https://flairsandglairs.in/
          https://flairsandglairs.com/

Ishani Agarwal

(Co-Founder- Flairs and Glairs)

Ishani Agarwal hails from the City of Joy, Kolkata.

She is the co-founder of her Community "Teekhe Zasbaaat" and Flairs and Glairs Publication.

Been a Compiler for 45+ Anthologies, she is in the process for more. Co-authored in 150+ Anthologies. She is a India Book of Records Holder, a Vajra World Records Holder, a High Range of Records Holder, an OMG Book of Records Holder, a Bravo Record holder, a Forever Star Book of World Records and an Indian Book of Records Holder.

Approved by Ne8x for its Lit Fest 2020, and Literary Icon 2020. Also a Golden Star Awards Winner 2020.

She has also been awarded with India Star Republic Award 2021, a part of She Awards by Awards Arc and Winner of Nari Samman 2021 by Literoma.

She is also selected as Best Achiever of the Year by AwardsArc and Most Challenging Compiler Award by Spectrum Awards.
She got her first solo Published,a solo Compilation consisting of first 750 contents of hers, titled "Hand That Burnt While Healing".

She has been featured by the National Magazine "Taree Zameen Par" with the title 'unstoppable'.
Also featured in the International Magazine DeMode for her upcoming solo novel, she is proud to write on social issues, and is happy with the love she is receiving.
Connect with her on Instagram: @Ishani_agarwal_quotes / @compilations_so_far

Shivangi Gupta
(Compiler)

My name is SHIVANGI GUPTA. I have completed my MBA from HR and MARKETING. I wrote a book that is available on amazon "Love In 3 Heart attack". I have also compiled a book 'SPUR ON'. If you like my content do contact me on instagram @shivangicv3; cv__writes

# Time Passed And Now I Am Old!!!

I REMEMBER WHEN I WAS A KID

with a tension free life
A smile with silly wipe
No children no wife
Food fun and hilarious sleeping times

But at some point
A thought of growing younger
Was stuck into my eyes
I also thought growing young will give me a better life...

I REMEMBERE WHEN I GOT YOUNG

Family and friends
schooling and trends
Tension of exams
But still lot of fun

But at some point
A thought of getting mature was seen like shining bright sun
May be being mature is better than being young

I REMEMBER WHEN I GOT MATURE

family tension with a relation tension
College friends were now competition
With a business creation
Settlement was on focus
Dreams were lost
Night sleep were less mentioned!!!

But at some point
A thought of getting married
Looked to relieve all my tension

I REMEMBER WHEN I GOT MARRIED

two bodies 1 soul
Two people 1 dreams
Two discussions 1 solutions
Now everything had a different situation
  THOUGHTS OF KIDS

later on blessed with two kids
Gave everything to them
And I started counting beads
They grew up
And my life is now at last stage
Almost free

At this point
Just one thought
Instead of enjoying the best
I focused the rest

Live the current stage
Live every age
Its the best YOu won't get it back

ENJOY THIS PHASE
OR YOU WILL REGRET AT DYING STAGE

Vasvi Ganjoos

@sseellccoouutthh
Someone who wants to portray her emotions through words.
The reason I write is for people to relate.

Respected People Of Society

Men can cry too and that's totally alright. Let's make the world comfortable enough for men to express their emotions. May be we were too naïve to understand this but they do have feelings that need to be manifested. Out there in the society," men do not cry" is a taboo that has led many men feel that no matter what the situation they need to be apathetic. Crying should not be considered a sign of fragility (as people think it is). As one who is capable of expressing their emotion is the strongest.

Irrespective of our gender, we all need regards. It shouldn't matter if it's a guy or it's a girl, social restriction has never proved beneficial for mental health of any being. It's totally okay and very nice gesture to praise men, admire them. They too deserve to be loved immeasurably, pampered like babies, empathized when upset. All of what is considered non masculine should have been disregarded long when we all have men in our lives (whatever relation it may be) and we all know how much they struggle in order to express their sentiment. Let's together make this world a wonderful place to live in where no matter what gender you are you van feel and show your emotions. Let us all adore all the special menin our lives. Tell them how lucky you feel about their their presencein your life. Men too need to be taken care of. They may hesitate to tell us what they are going through but we must be patient enough with them 'cause girls they haven't been treated this way'. They too have scar that they always try to hideand don't want anyone to know about because in our society men crying over issues has never been considered normal. Life is tough for all so let's stand for each other.

We can never imagine what a mess could be up there in those mind which cant even express what they are going through. It must be exhausting and grueling for them. Why nor appreciate them for always standing strong besides us in whatever relation it may be. Lets relieve them fron their burden and help them to express and communicate about what they feel. After all we all are together in this.

Yash Sarohiwal

Insta _allthatiwrite_
I am not a writer just a guy who know how to express itself.

<u>Love</u>

Love is the most beautiful emotion,
Wouldn't it be easy if their was a potion;
When you feel amazing ,
When you fondly admire this fascinating feeling,
Dude its just the beginning;
Its not as good as it seems,
Some times consequences are broken hearts and dreams;
There are fight, there are changes.
It require forgiveness and understanding to go ages;
You have to keep your ego aside its not always about
yourself,
Wish love was pure as love itself.

<u>Modern Relationship</u>

Yes, we wanna be loved,
Whilw looking for lust around us;
We appreciate the unkind body rather than the kind soul,
After all its worth if it isn't Instagram couple goals;
We connect online to feel an actual connection,
While in nudes and sext we seach for affection,
We swipe left in order to find the right one,
We want to win the marathon , whilw being scared to run;
We don't label relationships, we run when it gets serious,
We don't want relationship, while craving for one,
isn't it mysterios?

Aniket

insta handle : @aniket.writer
myself:
hello friends my name is Aniket dhiman. I am a small citien of dev bhoomi himachal Pradesh who is very fond of writing. I ll put some things related to my life here in front of you through poetry . hope you all like it. And don't forget to join on my Instagram for more of my poem

Ab jab jab aakh lagaoge tum
Mujhko khwaab me paoge tum

Naa paani hai naa hai ret yahan
Is aag ko kaise bhujhaoge tum

Tumne toh tasweerein samhaal rakhi hai
Mujhko kaise bhulaoge tum

Mere naam ki ab arzi mat karna
Khuda ke ghar jab bi jaoge tum

Rok deta hai har ghadi dimaag
Mujh tak kaise ab aaoge tum

Jazbaat ban chukka hun anchaha ek
Mujhe andar hi ander dabaoge tum

Mai mar jaun duaayein karoge
Meri hi jhoothi kasmein khaoge tum

Daba kar dard-e-gam kitna jiya hun main
Jaan jaoge toh bhut pachtaoge tum.
Tera mera jo khoosoorat na ho
Aisa koi pal nahi tha

Maana ke hum galat hain
Shod jaana koi hal nahi tha

Dooriyaan karne se agar tumhe
Rahat milti hai toh yahi sahi

Maine bhahut socha tha yaara
Aisa nahi hamara kal nahi tha

Aditi Bohra

Insta; aditi_a_
She is a enthusiastic girl who wants to fulfil her dreams with
her write-ups
She tries to write everyday something good.

I never thought I ll never fall again
Everyone sees me struggling to myself
But you won't see me fall
Regardless if I'm weak or not
I am going to stand tall
I am going to give biggest smile
Even though I want to cry
Am going to fight to live

Even though I am destined to die

I learned the difference between
Delusion and real love
For I've been deceived
So many times before
By life
Be people
Be my own instincts
By the world
You may see struggle though it all
But wont see me fail

Why are we so afraid
To fall in love?
Is it the hurt, the heartbreak,
Or not being enough?
Why are we so afraid
To even try?
To take a risk, to jumpto soar
To fly?
But in this lifetime
I cant seem to say
I'll find someone who'll stay

I am definetly broken , my heart is broken, but I will stand back
and live my life, I will love again yes I will fall again.

Dattasmita Hebburu Vishwanath

an avid, creative writer and lyricist , and serving as IT manager. As knowledge seeker presented many papers and attented national, international conference, seminars and workshops and authored the book, the light journey towards serene {ISBN 978-93-5279-517-8}.

Handled session for personality development. The interests include ndian culture, religion, philosophy and exploring the imbibed heritage. She has been honored with the accolades and awards during her endeavors. The most recent award "being young kasshachiever award "for her research on big data. She has also been awarded second prize for her well performed drama under creative theme in National level audition

<u>Behold!</u>

Slower the eyes;
Open the gates,
Will never graces,
You a witch mate.

Fasten the sight,
Strengthen the fate,
Allowthe waves,
Can behold the braves'

Farthest the destiny,
Serene the crown,
Regret the affinity,
Towards the frowns.

Smoother the journey,
In the mist grey,
Behold the success,
At the gateway.

<u>Admire</u>

Nor the end,
Its seemless journey,
Shall i begin,
By admiring you!

Though the words,
Never etiquette the glossary,
Shall I afford
By admiring you!

Gardening a gay,
Never hides a prey,
Shall I bequeath,
By admiring you!

Though the silence,
Never erase the fragnance,
Shall I behold,
By admiring you!

Though the hands,
Seems hidden in sands,
Shall I ahead
By admiring you!

Swetha Reddy

@the_hummingbirdo
Just another introvert who wants to make her own fairy tale.

<u>Izhaare-E-Mohabbat</u>

Kuch pal aise guzar gye
Jaise asmaan me baadal,
Jin me sirf baatein hi nahi,
Kuch yaadein bhi thi.
Darr tha hame mohabbat se is kadar,
Kahin hum apne aap ko na baithae,
Par uske saath ne,
Hamme apne aap se mila diya.
Hum yun jyada baatein krte nahi
Par wo jab sath ho hum rukhte hi nahi,
Bas yun samajh lena
Humko unse juda rehna acha lagta nahi.
Zindagi ne ek mauka diya
Aapko humse milne k liye
Par kuch aisa hua,
Hum aapse aise chipak baithe,
Jaise til tan par.
Ishq wala love jab unse hua,
Toh dil mil me jaane kya kya hua,
Unki aakhein dekhte hi,
Humne unme apna ashiyana bana liya.
Aajnabi the pyaar hone se pehle,
Aur pyaar hone k baad,
Aapne aapko ajnabi samjh baithe,
Kyuki apke siva hume kuch aur soojhta hi nahi.

Nidhi

Hi, I am Nidhi, a teacher by profession . I have a passion for writing since my teenage. Poetry for me has always been the best means to express my emotions. I am a logophile and possess a prolivity for writing poetry.
@nidhijsr

The Sprouting Ardour

I was there deep within,
And my life was to begin.
With the fall of mesmerizing rain,
I was ready to leave my domain.

And when the heavenly ray was shown,
With a bliss , I was born.
I came out in the world so pure,
Beautiful it would be, I was sure.
Now I got the heavenly heat,
And with my peers I could meet.
I learned to dance with the breeze,
And got an inspiration from the trees
That I would also grow up one day
To give the shades and be fay.
I'll learn to give without any demand,
And all the love that god will command.

I'll BE THERE FOREVER

When the sun will shower
Its ambrosial rays on you,
I'll be there and feel the warmth in you.
When you'll see the blooming flowers,
I'll be its fragrance and give you power.
When your life would be getting rough,
I'll be your strength and make you tough.
When you'll walk alone in the sand,
I'll be their holding your hand.
When you'll be happy with all the grace,
I'll be the smile on your face.
I'll be their in your thoughts,
I'll be there in your dreams.
I may be alive or may die,
I'll be always there just nearby.

Vaibhav Kumar Dwivedi

@vampire_talks
A guy filled with gratitude. Believes in healimg peple through own words and by taking withthem. Want to become a vamoire someday.

Unleashing Emotion

Here we are
Not together far apart
I'm so silly here
You quite smart

My words went in vain
You never felt the pain
Your eyes used to glow
Now tears use to flow

We were meant together
Pr you were not my part
I still don't know
Why we are apart

My words are dull
Brain lashing out of skull
Life going wrong
Still standing strong

No way to go
Nor a chance to turn
I hope I will not
Chose to return

As your love is a blessing
Which keeps me alive
Maybe not this then
In some other life

<u>Ittefaq</u>

Ittefaq ni h meri mohabbat
Warna kabki khatam ho gyi hoti
Imaan h mera
Marte dam tak sath degi teri namajudgi
Teri khamoshi
Mera intezaar
Mera kam hota waqt
Sab kismet ka khel nahi
Meri khud ki chuni dastan hein

Akanksha Bawa

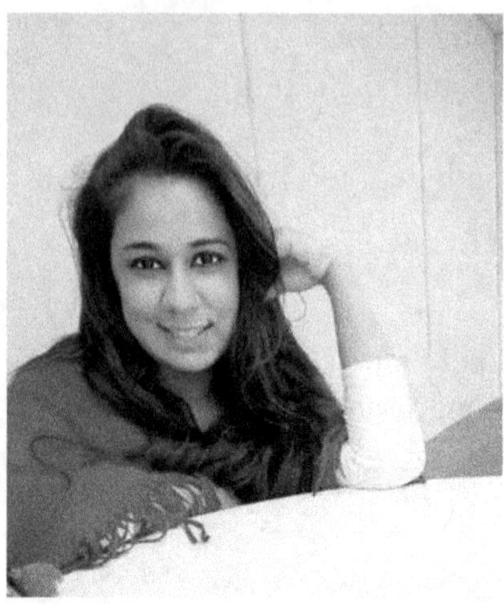

I am a certified life coach. I aspire to inspire others through my ideas , beliefs, words and everything I do. I wish to support people in living their best life by finding their purpose of being . I promote the fact of universe that every thing is energy and with law of attraction we can attract the lives of our dreams @affirm_manifest

<u>Self Love Is The Key</u>

I call it a heart break, not a breakup.
I always knew I am a self love queen until I got heartbroken. It was harsh and unbearable. In short, I lost myself. My life became like a melancholy song at every moment of my life.

I was afraid to unite those broken pieces . I was anxious so much with the mental trauma that I doubted will I be ever able to get myself back!

Healing took a lot of time for me to accept and let go. I finally started realizing how strong is the power of self love. I need not lose myself to keep anyone in my life. I stitched together my pieces back with gold.

People will try to break you down , tear you off, but you always keep your value!

I've fallen in love allover again with myself like never before. I foumd myself back and this time I promse to myself that I'm going to let myself down and feel frozen at any point in my life.

I now know the best investment I've ever made in investing in myself.

Love yourself, invest in youself- you won't regret it.

Utkarsha Phirke

Hello , I am utkarsha phirke. I am an MBBS student who happens to be good at words.

<u>The Thorny Love</u>

His entry in her life was like a pleasant sunrise,
He was one of her life's prettiest surprise!

He made her feel like a firefly,
He was the only one on whom she could rely!

But their was lack of serendipity in her story to experience love,
The fault in her stars broke her heart's cove!

His love for someone else was like a shinning jade,
Realizing this, her hopes of a 'forever' started to fade!

And thus the thorns of her unrequited love pricked her soul,
Leaving her mourning in dolour's buring coal!

<u>The Hatred</u>

I hate that moment when you sailed in my life,
unsnarling my every issues, resolved my inner strife!

I hate that moment when you gave me your shoulder to cry on,
Snuggling me, you tricked me in your charm's con!

I hate that moment when your perfect life skills left me bedazzled,
Without any second thoughts, I was ready to jump into your heart's puzzle!

I hate that moment when everything reminds me of you,
Cruising back inti the past, 'holding you' is the only thing I want to do'!

I hate that moment when I knew loving you is not an option
Even though I feel anguished, I am entrapped in this emotion.

Akash Malhotra

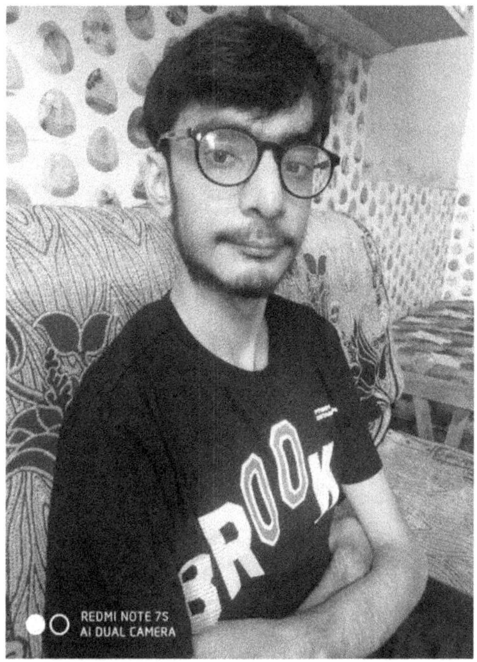

I am Akash Malhotra from lucknow, UP. I like to express myself through writings.

Pyaar

Karte hai pyaar ke daave kayi
Par samjhe na koyee matlab uska sahi
Koyee samjhe jismani sambhand ise
Tou koyee samjee svarth seedhe karne ka saadhan maatra
Pyaar tou vo hai jo ho ruhani
Na ho jalan , guroor ya hawas jahan
Na hi ho mere tere ki bhavna
Samman samjh ho jahan aapsi
Vhi hai pyaar sacha
Na hi koi vaisi duji bhavna

My How To –Poem

How to live?
It's what we learn from scriptures
How to love truly?
It's what we learn from SITA-RAM and RADHA –
KRISHNA holy pairs
How to deal with problems strongly?
It's what we learn from Lord RAM and Lord KRISHNA'S
life
How to make other realise?
By being an example of others

Suresh V.S

Guitarist , drummer

To the one whom I can't convey my love
 I don't know why you mean so much to me. I don't know why I get angry if you didn't talk. I don't know to convey my feelings to you. I don't know why I love you so much. I don't why the days I spent with you are the most beautiful days of my life. I don't know why I met you. I am not able to tell anything because I know this is not a dream. I am just stuck like a statue. You have become a desire of my heart. I don't know why this heart always carves for what I can't have. But the thing in my heart, my eyes will convey to you. Even when we are close we have a huge distance between us. My dreams with you are in my eyelids slowly crawling down my cheeks as tears. You're always with me but still you are not mine. These are my grievances for you. You can't be mine. I can't afford to lose you but still I don't know how to tell you. But in my dreams you will be always mine. I just hope that my nights last forever so that I can have you forever
Null

<u>Oh My Poor Heart</u>

Why do you always crave for the things that will never happen? Why do you always feels for something that never going to hppen? Why do you always feel for something that never going to happen ? why do you always care for something that never even know that we exist? Why do you always like the thing that never will be mine? Why do you keep repeating the same mistake? Why do you don't how control the feeling?why?

<u>My Love</u>

When I die . don't cry for me and don't bring any flowers to my grave , okay? I am allergic and I am tired of being left alone and not being loved. Loneliness is tough on my soul and contempt cuts my hearts. I don't know how to overcome you. A love is supposedly worth dying for. This damned words have been tattoed on your souls. The love that hurts is supposed to be true love. Love that despairs, that exasperates , that messes with our mind and creates a battle between the mind and heart, that turns us into shit. I don't know why the fuck we choose the wrong one all the time. Why do we always want the love that tear us apart? It teaches that pain is fun. But it hurts. And again we have to learn how to love. And that's how the life has to go on.

The night mare of our love
The nights where we don't know what to do. Where our thoughts will be wandering somewhere. Where we lie down and just think of a person who are not meant for us. And feel fpr people who never cared for us. Where our pillows will get wet. Where my dreams kills me and her smile haunts me and torchers us. I miss the time where nights were for sleeping.

My love,

When I die please come to my grave as a epitaph write your name on my tombstone so that I will be resting in peace by hugging your name.

To the one who pushed into the darkness and made me carry a heavy heart:

It's all my fault for trusting you with my full heart . its my fault , for giving u all the priority . its my fault , for making u the important person of my life . you taught me the important lesson of life "trust". You made me realise that "everythimg that glitters is not a gold". U thought that' in love promises are made to be broken". You left me with the scars that will never heal. I just realized that you didn't love me the same way I did. I am the one who held up on our relationship. Thankyou for the lessons you taught.

Jahnavi

My name is Jahnavi
I'm an extrovert and introvert with limited edition who always love to motivate others with my writings
I'm passionate in writing poems
It doesn't matter whether it is dark or bright , my self motivation never dies

<u>Introbeings</u>

A sacred knot by the soul of neonate with divine
A grip of quite sobbing connected with blood to soul

   INNOCENCE RUSHED OUT OF PAIN

Outmost footsteps under the lap of canopy
Baby step reaching the independent minds

INNOCENCE TURNED INTO MATURITY

Era of life became trainer
Experiencing thoughts elevation
Actions were crouching
Confuse surroundings
Endeavours the life of purity
Diffident heart with apt secrets

UNDERSTANDING TURNED INTO COHERENCE

Circumstances switched the true life
Incredible moral power of   voice
The wholly life with intense breath
Fear bliss, rolls down
Recalling the celestial introbeing.

Walk with me till…
My smile dazzle in your eyes
Walk with me till…
My choice have chance to express
The word 'I' changes to 'us'
Walk with me till…
Our pinky promises follows the unbroken words
Walk with me till…
You feel my tears in the rain
Walk with me till…
My breath synchronize to you touch
Walk with me till…
The littlest fingers embrace pure hearts
Walk with me till…
The moon shining out of its soul.

Shivangi Sharma

A 24 year old indourban strong headed sapiosexual humanbeing, comes from the city of nawabs , lucknow.
Taveller by passion, HR by professional.
She started by writing an article in the year 2015 for the topic "is marriage an end to career life" which has been recently published in a local newspaper name kisaan satta.

Started writing poetry and small open letters this year, one poem has been submitted to a government approved MSME by the name of "2 am thought" and the other is published with the velocity of thoughts.
She loves travelling to the mountains , weekend gateways to places like risshikesh and Jaipur have been accomplished by now.

Kosish Ki Tumhe Manane Ki

Kosish ki thi tumhe manane ki
Ek ek din pass na aane ki
Kosish ki tumhe apni chahat na banana ki…
Par tum mane nahi…
Par tum mane nahi aur hum haar se gye
Aur hum haar se gye kuch is kadar ki..
Kosish krne lage tumne manane ki
Har pal har lamha…
Ek ek din pass ane ki
Ek ek din pass aane ki…

Swastik Sharma

I am swastik sharma a budding writer and my forte is pantoum and limerick type of poetry. My Instagram id is swas_writes3 and I am pursuing my bachelor of arts degree from galgotias universi

<u>Wonder</u>

Do you still wonder?
Why you left my side and made me look like a guy who for one reasons cry.
Or it is because someother guy always hade your side.
Or I was the one who made you feel like the end will be a good bye.
Or is there any other reason because of which you didn't want to drop by.
May be the whole things makes you want to just stop wanting to try to get a good guy or is there any better way to tell this lie.

<u>Cry</u>

Why did I cry?
Maybe because after my still u went for that other guy.
Why did I cry?
Maybe because I was the one afterall who didn't lie.
Why did I cry?
May be because our relationship was the one thing to whom I didn't wanted to say goodbye.
Why did I cry?
Maybe bcause now I was the one left dry.

Kashish Jain

@kasishjainwriter

Her Red Lips Revealing One Evidence

That she eats my soul
Her blue eyes exhibition
"a magic world"
The world where many people are inhabited
But now it showing a bigger vacancy of one person
I think now, she targeting me
My black shirt she throws on the bed
And then kisses me on my chest
I touch the floor
But she pulls me up
I try to refuse her plan
But she still kisses me on my lips.

Suddenly I entered her world
I: where I am?
That women : "welcome to the magic world"
The world which runs on my hands.
 And you just do
What I want from you
"welcome to my magic world"
As I already told you
"her lips are evidence that she eats my soul"
Second:
Every petal of rose defines you
The fragrance of rose help me to determine you
You're my rose and
I'm your leaves
Our bond is so pure
And so sweet
Your skin tone is red
And mine is green
 I think this the best combination

People have ever seen
Honey, more often I also
See that everyone
Loves you so much
And they symbolize you
As a queen of expressing love
And why not?
Cause you are a rose.
But sometimes, I hate this
Being your leaf , it also makes sense
That I only have the right to love you.
Honey,you are my life
And you're my strength without rose
This leaf is nothing without a rose
These leaves will come soon to the end.

Bhavya Khanna

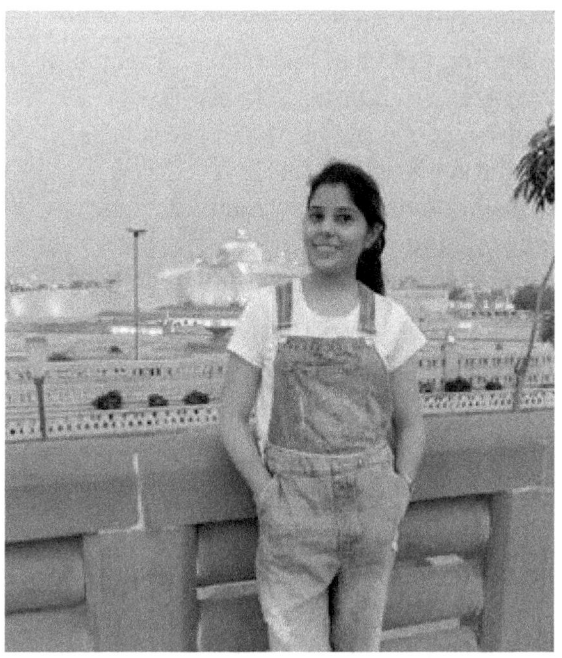

Lucknow
Pursuing law
She is an ambivert and an avid reader. Books have been her best friends ever since and writing is her weapon of expressing her thoughts and feelings
@bhavya_khanna11

<u>The Special Someone</u>

Life never stayed the same
It was for the first time that I learned your name
There was aggravation, there was this heat
We stood viz a viz and my heart skipped a beat
Our eyes bored for the first time…
It was that instant when I knew you were mine
Thing went by at their own pace
You became my past, present, future and it was such an alluring phase
You were the perfect one you were astute
I was eccentric always bemused
You made me believe in the beauty of life
Standing beside you was everything that I desired
Having you by my side i feel blissful everyday
We walk all the road together, is all that I pray
Holding your hand , walking side by side
I feel content I feel that pride
A fairy tale romance is not what I desire
Those extra little efforts is all that I admire
You lift me up when I lose all hopes
Rescuing me every time I slither ' cause of the phoebes'
The ups and downs… the sorrows and the frowns
We pass every test , we know no bounds
Life is beautiful it plays it's game
The day you held my hand life never stayed the same…

Sanjeev Kumar

He is a professional tax consultant, CA student and a writer. He is very keen on writing and expressing through the power of words. He believes that a piece of waste if it does not motivate someone. His school of thought is to bring irony in the real-life scenerios and pen them down in a simple way.

@rndm_thoutz

Love

(a) For them "you are one in a million"
But for me "you are the only one."

(b) It's not about "finding the one you deserve"
It's about finding the one "who deserve you".

(c) The specialty of our love is,
We know the fact that we won't be together
Yet we are madly in love with each other.

(d) She is so busy in playing demon,
She forgot, she used to be an angel.

(e) She let him inside of her heart,
He chose to be there forever as love.

(f) She let him dive into the depth of her heart,
And he drowned in the feeling of it.

(g) The corner of her heart is the place,
Where he met the happiest version of himself.

(h) You don't need to tell,
I can see it in your eyes

<u>"Move On "& "Motivation"</u>

(a) Do love passionately , not blindly.

(b) Just remember how they treated you, you won't need any
    other reason to move-on.

(c) "love" be careful with it,
    Once it is done wth you,
    You won't be the same again.

(d) "reality" eventually it will hit you,
     So be careful
    Because when it,
    It won't be easy for you.

(e) Not always you need a closure from your partner,
    Sometimes self-closure is sufficient enough to move-on.

(f) Just forgivethem,
    Pain will go away by itself.

(g) You are broken,
    But universe have mysterious ways to fix.

Shri Dakshayani

She is shri dakshayani from Hyderabad.
She says, she finds her soul when she writes and enjoys putting emotions to words. She loves writing short stories and quotes .she always believe to defeat the defect before the defect defeats you.

@tangled_notions
shridakshayani@gmail.com

- Someone asked what is the most difficult task?
  "to unlove him" I replied

- What's your secret of being so happy these days, he asked
  When I am with you I am adding life to my days not days
  to my life,she smirked.

- Do you love sweets, she asked
   He said, I hate sweets except one
  The girl blushes while he said the only sweet I love is your
  sweet little soul.

- I can make out how your heart feels and the depth of your
  love
  Your beautiful moking eyes everything in…

- You gaze at the moon
  I gaze at you…
  You're my moon
  We both gaze at what we love the most
  I love you

- While she was whining with grief this girl stands by her
  and fills in her heart with love stating I'm here with you
  always and forever.

- Oh dear!!!
  We shouldn't love someone so much that we can't even
  feel ourselves
  Making us void…
  Love youself like you love them
  Refill yourself with your love

- Let your heart and soul taste the magic of your own love.

- I looked at myself in the mirror and thought

  "why am I so terrible at handling myself and getting myself together!!?
  This is not what I deserve,
  I smiled and said…
  Mirror mirror on the wall!!

  The most happiest person on earth will be me from this moment.

  HAPPY ME!!!

- I Woke up too early…
  I couldn't get back to sleep again.
  I made a cup of coffee for myself and sat in our corridor
  What a bliss!!! To experience the raindrops patting on my legs with a cool breeze making me cold with a warm coffee.
  It made my day…felt amazing … the ME time I got , after many days.

- I met my grandma after a long time
  She dyed her hair today
  She was very happy and started mocking mom about her grey hair.
  Such a precious heart… felt like she's a kid…
  May be that's why they say old people are like babies.

Aakrati

Hey !! this is aakrati
I always played well with words and here I am writing poems
and getting myself published

<u>Princess In A Cage</u>

HUSH!!! Girls please don't say,
With whom you had to forcefully lay,
Because that would lead to shrinking and curl,
Of your family's reputation as pure as pearl.

Hush!! Girls please don't fight,
Let your talents burn in flames of light.
Because for that you need to step out of houses,
Leading your family into debtness and losses.

Hush!!girls please learn to hide your sigh,
Lower down your ambitions and don't fly high.
Because that will lead to a path laden with golds,
So it seems better to others if you hide within folds.

Sometimes it's just a simple request you made,
That forced you to regret and use the blade.
I've seen crying with shrills,
Ending up life by falling from hills.

But there's still not present a sign of shame,
And everyone answers that girls are to be blamed.
So dear princesses who are trapped in a cage,
It's now your turn to show the rage.

<u>402.9 Miles</u>

A distance far enough to cover,
To console and hug your lover,
Siting there and talking sometimes doesn't heals,
Because the other has the chance to hide what he feels.

While the one pretends to be alright,
The other uses the pillow at night,
To dry all the tears and act tomorrow fine,
All feelings are jumbled up like a grape vine.
Don't know where to go,
Don't know where to stay,
This is how we spend our day,
&this is how we spend our day.

Sandhiya Mani

An engineer by profession
A writer by passion
An artist by interest
Chocolates is something I don't share
Challenges is what I always dare
Himalayan trekking is my lifeline ambition
Awaits for the miracles to happen
Nature is the only love of my life
Simplicity is the character I hold
Naughty acting makes me bold
Self respect is something I never sold
I do what I love and love what I do
First cried on 2nd rook of 8th grid took a move
Known to the world as SANDHIYA MANI.

Life Changeover

Born as caterpillar and living in the world,
I have been avoided by many people.
I wished to own someone as my owner
And be their favorite pet.
My beauty seemed ugly to the world
And my greasy body texture
Was not liked by anyone around me.
Longing for some love and care,
I was waiting all my life.
Just when I was clinging onto the leaf
Upside down totally depressed,
I felt some changes in my body.
Surprised to my reflection in water,
Got stunned with the way I changed.
Having changed to an attractive creature,
Gained attention of the world towards me.
My every single wish to get love
Was getting fulfilled
When my wings ejected out from my body
And I stared to fly as butterfly.

Feel The Warmth

A regular walk at night
Wandering round the streets
With out of words to talk
Listening to each other's heartbeat
Where our hands longing to unite
Taking every step forward
Being in a comfort zone
And the world holding us
Together as one!

Priyanshi Pragya

The fascinating girl you are reading about is PRIYANSHI PRAGYA.

She resides in sahibganj district of Jharkhand.

For the time being she lives in ranchi, doing graduation in horticulture.

The set of circumstances led her to express her thoughts through writing.

The framework of the society captivates her attention. She loves writing on social topics.

Besides this, singing dancing and crafts are her fascination.

She dreams to be a civil servant and serve for her motherland. Her one and only aim is to make her family and country proud…

Writing – A Process

Writing is not just writing
It's a difficult process of engraving
Some master pieces
Made up of most
Intellect conclutions
On something.

Will You Be My Love

Yes!! I can be the mercury for you
Who will share the warmth of love amazingly.

Yes! I can be the VENUS who can do every small things to fill your life with shine.

Yes!! I can be the EARTH. Who will definitely pamper & inspire you always.

Yes!! I can be the MARS who will try to decorate your path with red petals of flowers by all possible ways.

But let me know first
Would you like to be my universe?

Proposal Of Love

I Know that you are broken inside.

I assure that I will patiently
Accept the broken pieces
And aggregate them to
Make a happy soul again.

Irony

Though the size of a raindrop
And tear
Is almost same

So isn't ironical that
We can hold
Thousand of raindrops
Showered on our eyes
But can't hold a
Single drop of tear.

Susmita Roy

Hello this is susmita roy who is living in Kolkata.
Currently pursuing her last year of bcom.
She love to describe her feelings through write-ups. Which can directly relate t reader's emotion
@susmitaroy_

Yaad aa raha hai
Wo tera mujhe dekh kar has dena
Kai angina bematlab ishaza tera
Mujhe yaad aa araha h

Janti hu benaam is riste ko mod tay nahi hai
Pay kya karu tere sath dekha har sapna yaad aa raha hai…

Kasmein wadein saare isme tujhe yakeen kaha hai
Isliye to bin phero ke tujhe apna banaya hai…

Mat karo wada mujhse milne ka hume manzoor hai
Magar dil par mere sirf ab tera hi suroor hai…

Aitbaar hai beshumaar hai, apse jyada aapse pyaar hai,
Bayaan karu kaise mai ki ye hua kaise hai..

Bas itna keh du tujhe ke mere liye tu itna kimti hai
Mol na de pau tera kabhi, itna tu anmol hai…

Dooriyaan kaha bhula payengi tujhe, tu to mere dil me hai
Aur haa sach kahu to ab bhi teri har yaadon se pyaar hai…

Yaad aa araha hai
Aaj bhi tu waise hi
Kya kru ek tu hi toh hai
Dhoondhne pe ashique to kai milenge
Magar who teri mahek hum kaha se laenge
Tu kuch mere asmaan ke chand sa hai
Koi samjhega nahi isse , na kisiko samjhana hai
Bas tu jaan lena yahi kafi hai.

Ki aaj bhi tu hamein kuch aise hi yaad hai…

Tera who ek pal ka dekhna kafi hoga
Satana mujhe phir chupke se hasana kafi hoga,
Who be-wajah ladna tera
Bematlab ka jhagadna kafi hoga,
Kafi hongi who saari adhoori baatein bhi
O sayad chalti toh kabi khatam nahi hoti,
Magar kya kre hamare baton ka vakt kafi hoga,
Ab na tera who masoom sa gussa hoga,
Na tere aage koi bewajah rootha hoga,
Sab jaan leta than a tu bin bole
Phir bata tere jaane se mere hasr kya hoga…

Upar baitha khuda hume dekh toh raha hoga
Bharosa hai uspe who kuch soch kr rakha to hoga
Aisa kaise tod dega wo hume
Mannat me usne ek lauta manga jo mujhe hoga.

r

Soniya Negi

hey!! This is soniya negi
uttarakhand inshot you can call me shona.
Sarcasm is in my veins
@shonnaaaa_

Vo Tum

vo tumhari aakhein aur un aakhon se yun sharmana,
vo tumhara hoth or un hotho se yun muskurana,
vo tumhari kamar or us kamar se yun behlana,
vo poori tum aur tumhara yun ethlana

vo poori tum aur tumhara yun ethlana
mujhe beintaha pasand hai
mujhe beintana pasand hai tumhara yun sharmana

Khasra

Tum aao to sahi
Mohabat me chal rha khasra ghatao toh sahi,
Gairat hai tumhein dekh kar,
Kabhi huskar hume bulao toh sahi.

Daastae-E-Dil

Daastan-e-dil ki kya sunaye
Ayy galib jara hum bhi muskuraye!!
Pooch mat hote hai kitne sitam
Dil me hai toh bus-
Aane aur jaane wale ka gum.

Nemi Chand Mawari

Nemi chand mawari "nimay"Poet, writer and chemist.
Self written poetry books : "kavya ke phool-2013","anuragini-ek premkavya-2020", and 3rd book
"kohare ki aagoshi me" in publishing process.
Editor of an anthology "svapnmanjari-2020"
Fb page – Thestarpoet"nimay"
Insta ID : mawari_nimay
Prizes :" tulsidas sahitya samman -2013
"atal Bihari vajpeyi smriti samman -2020","2nd prize winner in state level poetry competition -2015"

Milta wahi hai jo bota hai
Ram ko ramzaan me pujun ,yak ahu nanak ko peer,
Banke yesshu sooli chad jaun, ya naino se bahaun neer.

Gali gali me dekh aadambar, dil har din ab rota hai,
jab sabko mitti me hai milna , to nit – nit kyu jhagda hota
hai?

Soone pade hai chaubaare, jahan radha urdu bola krti thi,
Chacha ki ek lauti poti, jahan tulsi ko seechan krti thi.

Gurudwaare ki prasaadi khane, jahan john bhi jaya karta tha
Amandeep bhi churc me, jaakar mattha tikaya karta tha.

Jab gangaur ,Diwali or eid ko, mikar sath manaate the,
Bade dino ki chutti kahkaar , sab Christmas par mauj manate
the.

Geeta ki kasmein kha kr all ki azaanen hoti thi,
Zend-awesta ko padhkr, nanakvaani ki kami poori hoti thi.

Magar samay ne karwat lekar, nafrat ka jahar hai ghol diya,
Ek dooje ke dvesh bhav ne , dharm ko palade par taul diya.

Vish ghula hai saampradayikata ka, insaan kaha chain se sota
hai,

Par ek din pachtaenge hum sab, kyuki milta wahi hai jo bota
hai.,
Ek dooje ke dvesh bhav ne , dharm ko palade par taul diya.

Vish ghula hai saampradayikata ka, insaan kaha chain se sota
hai,
Par ek din pachtaenge hum sab, kyuki milta wahi hai jo bota
hai.

Chetan

Apna kahke fir mukra , mere bas ki baat nahi,
Aasamaan se tare lane ki meri khud aukaat nahi.
Mai mitti me pala badha , bus baat jameen ki karta hun,
Aabad basti ka banjara hu , majboor hun thoda , barbaad nahi.

Choti-choti khusiyon k pal samet kanjali men Rekhta hun,
Gurzi ban chehre ki muskanon ka, pal pal aage badhta hun.

Rangmanch ki adla-badli ka pass mere koi raaj nahi,
Ek vazeer hun keval apne khel ka, koi raja ka taaz nahi.

Man ki maanun bas man ki karta hun,
Ye manmaan hai koi chaal nahi.
Fakkad se satrangi mera mausam , jismen bijli ki kadkadaahat
nhi.
Meethi –meethi bearish peeta hun, sailabon ki kadvaahat nahi,
Aadam hun aadam ki jaati ka, koi ukhda hua shaitaan nahi.
Apni aadat roz badalna mera bus ki baat nahi…

Shubhashree

FROM MDURAI, TAMIL NAIDU, INDIA
She is much interested in literature and wishes her contribution to linguistic education with evidence based research and in future to collaborate with academics both in India and around the world.

Sheela's Life

Sheela is a 20 years old girl living with her parents, ram and priya. Both of her parents are working as school teachers. She is their only daughter and she enjoys her life living with them. As she belongs to upper class family , she has some limitations. She could not spend more time with her family as there are busy with their work.

They both come late at home after completing their work at school.they have only a little amount of time to spend with their daughter. Mostly she is alone. She has only few friend to share feelings and emotions. Many a times she ask her parents to go for the part time job. But they don't allow her to goo for the part time job. After coming from college , she chats with her friends through whatsapp messages and she visits her facebook page. Apart from this she talks with her friends during her free time through mobile phones. Rarely she meets her friends and goes shopping with them. Only during holidays she goes to watch movies with her friends, she doesn't find anything interesting in her daily routine. She loves to be lonelness but sometimes she gets bored because of lonely feeling. She wants to share her feelings with others. But her family members are bus with their work and her friends are not so close to her.though she belongs to the upper class family she is not living a happy life.

"sheela's life represent the modern women of our society"

Many of us think mone is everything but we fail to understand that there are manythingswhich are valuable than money in our lifes. Friends and relatives are the personwho form the major part of our life. An individual can share his feelings with his close friends and relatives . but today we don't give importance to relatives and friends. We don't spend much time with our parents. Instead we give importance to money and wealth in our life. Even a rich girl like Sheela is not happy because she has everything except happiness.

"Family and friends make happiness in our life".

Shalini

@shalu_qveen

There are two things
1 to defeat…
2: to be defeated!!!

Choose what you do…

No matter how elder or younger
Everyone has something to learn on this earth
In the life till last day…

Earn such fame
That your diary
Change others life…
I can bring both
Suns fire and moon peace
Depends on you!!

Let all your failures
Be the story for your success!!
And let all the success be the story of your life…

Roshni Agrawal

She is Roshni Agrawal. She hails from delhi. She has been part of 20+ anthologies and many more are there in the compilation process she finds happiness in little things. She started writing in her school days. She writes quotes, snippets, musing but also loves to write poetry sometimes. She is philosophical and a simple girl who likes listening to old songs. She had done her graduation in double major in sociology-political science and diploma course in travel and tourism from Mumbai. The countries explored by her up till now is Australia , USA , Hongkong, Macau, Singapore , Malaysia.

<u>You Are The Epitome Of Love</u>

Believe in love
Because you are the one
Its there in your heart
Deep and intact.
Don't give punishment
To yourself by loosing it
No one is powerful
To take away your soul
From you with their
Misdeeds and misbehavior.

+

<u>A Divine Love</u>

Let me love you endlessly
With pure intention and selflessly
No amount of evil activities
Or difficulties can separate us
Because our love is profound,
Divine and guided by god.
You came in my life
Like a shooting star and
All my wishes got fulfilled.

Love Came From The Universe

LOVE is that dose
From the universe
Which tells someone is still there
From the above
To care.
You are not alone.

Life Is Beautiful

Life is neither too short nor too long
THE moment in which we are living is life,
Every breath which we are taking is life,
Everyday which we are celebrating ourselves is life,
Our deeds and action which we take is life,
Doing those things which makes us happy is life,
Life is described by the way of your living, life is the art of
living.

Manju PB

@_tapasvi_
I live in kochi

Black And White Mind

In this world of curiosity
Why are you hiding
Between the roots of life
Smile please
Thunder will give this light
For you to show your
Blissful moment to the world

In this freezing night
With the presence
Of moon and infinite stars
I saw you for the first and last time
Seized you in my fantasy of emotion
Won't see you ever
With my naked eyes
Will never gonna forget
Cause you're
Not an ordinary
You're beyond the universe like
BLACK AND WHITE.

A Journey To Insight

Rays of peace
Searched you in the illusonanary realm
Of magic mirror

I saw you in the dark
Fireflies were wandering
Their light splashed
Into your infinite soul

Eyes gone wild
Comet showed the way
Stay with me
Till doomday, dear me.

Krithika Unmesh

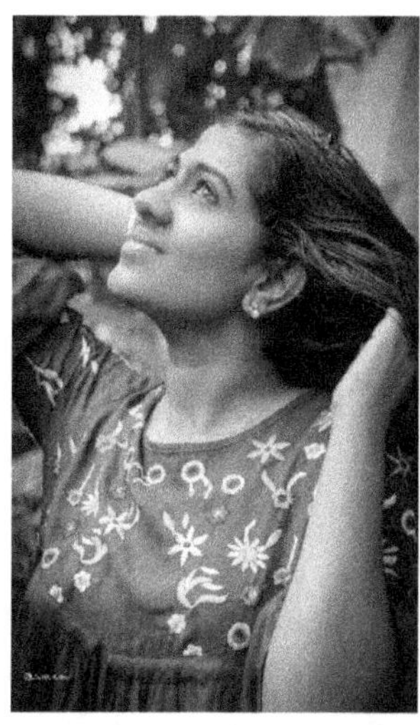

Krithika Unmesh is an aspiring writer and poetess, born in Quilon district of Kerala on April 23,1998. She writes for anthologies and on online writing platforms such as pratilipi, Instagram , few blogs etc. She is a budding researcher aka chemist and is currently pursuing integrated masters at Central University of Tamil Nadu, Thiruvarur. Apart from these , she is vehement to dance and have been trained bhartnatyam for many years.

"Five Feet Apart" Moment.

Thousand nerves congest within,
Quite frail and brittle;
It's hellish wintry.
I'm feeling cold,
Slowly numbing and deadly.
Be near , settle close,
Grab my frigid body.
Only your breath can warm me now.

Him

With his boisterous tone,
That crests from time to time,
And eyes shooting out into mine,
He gifted me everything he collected all day.
His firm hands narrated me everything he has explored.
He was excited about the world around him.
I was excited about his excitement.

(…isn't so exciting to listen to eccentric people telling you
how their day was!!! Dedicated these words to eccentric
people of your life.)

I Am Jealous

I am jealous of everyone who walked with you.
I am jealous of everyone who laughed with you.
I am jealous of every other breath that fell on you.
I am jealous of every ears that heard you.
I am jealous of every shoulders you embraced.
I am jealous of everything you kissed.
I am jealous of everyone who felt your lub-dub.
I am jealous of every heart that spilled your love.
Jealousy kills the beholder, they say.
Then why am I still breathing!!!!

Kaashvi

I'm kaashvi, I hanker to burgeon positivity and love in the world. Writing has always brought me ecstasy. I unveiled my poetry skills to connect with people more effectively and portray my thoughts and emotions aesthetically. Being a biophile is what I recommend and being dreamer is what I prompt for!

<u>The Immortal Love</u>

I look upto the sky wondering why, that you are with me, yet
I feel alone.
The wind feels heavy , the world feels lifeless,
The nights are darker, the days less brighter.
The tears shine in the starlight,
Oh Love… you were as beautiful as a twilight.
You were the strings to the guitars,
You were the moon among the stars,
Everyday with a hope I lay below the dark starry cover,
A shooting star will pass by for me to make a wish,
To bring you back to me , for me to attain a bliss,
Yet, i Know it will remain an unfulfilled wish.
And if you're looking at m from up there,
Oh… my love, take me with you.
For the Magics make no sense at me,
For the Happiness makes no sense to me,
For this Life makes no sense to me,
For this Universe make no sense to me without you…!!

Tharadara

She is Tharadara hakimafatema from Ahmedabad Gujrat. Currently she is pursuingher pharmacy degree from L.M college of pharmacy Ahmedabad, Gujrat. Part time she is working as a math's and science teacher in classes.

Apart from this , she is writer and craft person. For her writing is to introducing herself with words which work more than action.

Her quotes for writing"alfazo ki duniya me behas nai kalam chalti he".

She think, pendown emotion in words makes beautiful rythym to live life happily.

Her mother and her sister is her biggest inspiration.

Insta handle- @tharadara123hmt
tharadarafatemaofficial

Mohabbat Ka Saphar

Mohabat jindagi ka ek haseen lamha
Jisse ho jaye ban jaye vo poora jahaan
Sirf naam unka chehare pe muskaan lae
Vaisa hai ye aseem chanchal man ka dhuaan.

Ye vaqt har kisi ki jindagi mein aaya
Khud se jyada kisi or ki fikr laya
Ek pal use khud se dur na kiya jae
Apano se jyada dil ka azeez banaya

Behate paani ki tarah vaqt behane laga
Dobate ko tinke ka sahara milane laga
Jab koi apna na tha jindagi me aas pass
vo akela hi hame jindagi me kafi lagane laga
achiever
Andheri raat mein jaise koi suraj ban gaya tufano ke
samandae se ladane Himmat de gaya
bin kahi baato koYu aakhon se padh ke vo anjaan jo Tha
kabhi ,
 aaj dil ka hafiz ban gaya

Bar bar darta huva man use apnana Chahen
parivar ka ek ahem hissaBanana chaahen
samaaj aur logo Ki bctuki baton ke beech gumnam Dil
himmat samet uska hona chaahen

Vaqt jate har kisi ki yahi daastan Bani hai
 pyaar ke baad logo ki baate Nazar aai hai
ma-baap ki izzat ke khatir kisi ne khud
Apne hi pyaar ki kashti bekhasata duboi hai

Kuch fkhar dil ese bhi judate dekhe hai

Har khushi or gam saath saath jite hai
Jab saath lekr maa-baap ki dua-en
Apani jindagi ki nai shuroraat karate hai

Jaise doobate ko tinake ka sahara
Hota hai vaise ek sachcha hamsafar juroori hota hai
Dua hai meri har kisi ki mohabat ho poori
Saath rahe vo joda jo ek dusare ka hota hai…

Drishtant Maurya

I am drishtant maurya , it's been three years of my writing , and everyday I am aiming to improve it, and I have found that this pen and paper are the most convenient way to express myself to the audience out there, so it is my medium to communicate my heart out.

(1)

Aaj phir ye raat , taaro se saji hae,
Aur hamari mulakat, khyabo mein likhi hae,
Kuch baato ko bheja hein, in havao ke sath tumhari aur,
Par ab toh inhe bhi yeh bbaate bachkaani si lagne lago hein.

Yu toh chand bhi dikh jaata tha, ek amavas baad,
Par yaha toh barso se grehen ki rate guzri hein,
Aur iss ugte sooraj ke didar ke intezzar mae, roz dupta suraj
chhot ta ja rha hae,
Kai barishe aakr guzar gai,
Par ab tak savan na aa saka ha.

(2)

Phulo ka girna mere angan mein aam ho gya tha,
Uska guzarna meri gali se, ab roz ka ho gya tha.
Un phulo ko ikhetha kar rakhta hu aaj bhi,
Socha ha eek din guldasta banakar dunga tumhe , aur apni dil
ki baat kahunga tumse.

Yeh kuch bebuniyaadi baate hein, jo mae apne se hi karta hu,
Na toh tumhara naam Janata hu,
Na hi pata,
Bas in aakho pae bharosa karke iss dil ne guhar lagai hae,
Yeh jo ladki guzarti hae
Tere

Mitali Singh

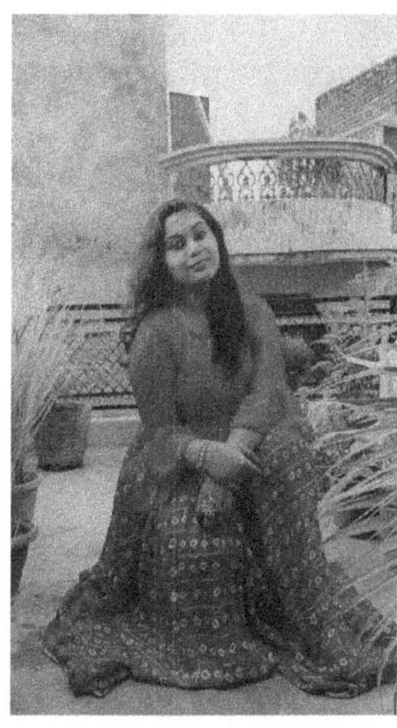

Mitali singh is from "city of nawabs" Lucknow, Uttar Pradesh. She is 19 year old girl. She is pursuing her bachelor's in visual Arts from techno institute of higher studies. She have always fall in love with colours since childhood which make her bring them together into her canvas. She loves to write up her emotions in her favorite diary since 2016, that make her an ameture writer which grows sher love of playing with words in the form of her poetries day by day. She feels when no one can understand your emotions its you who can understand you well and that can be enough to motivate yourself on every darkest time…. This will be her third compiled book so if you want to read her amazing work you can find her writing and art works and connect with her on Instagram
@kala_premi_
@shinystar_mits
Swtmitali22@gmail.com

<u>Dadi</u>

Who teri ungali pakad ke mera chalna
Gir padne par tera zameen ko marna
Who god mai tere mera bekhauf sojana
Babu kehkr tera mujhe uthana
Who haatho se tera mujhe khana khilana
Aasu behne par chup karwana
Who galti par mera kaan khichna
Par sabki daant se mujhe bachana
Who dhundhli si kuch yaadein teri
Who khatti – meethi baatein teri
Aaj bhi humesha bhut yaad aati hai
Dil mai teri yad bas ghar si kar jati hai
Kaash waqt ko thoda roka hota
Us ungli ko tera thaam ke
Maine vakt se kuch pal manga hota
Bharso baad bhi tee jane ka gam taza lagta hai
Tere na hone ka ehsaas dil ko adha krta hai
Kash laut aate who pal sabhi sath bitaye dadi
Teri beti ko aaj bhi tera yu door cale jaana ander hi ander bhut
rulata hai…

Dharam Mayne Rakhta Hai

Dharam mayne rakhta hai
Han dharam mayne rkhta hai
Society ke janjaal se logon ke bawal se
Dharam mayne rakhta hai
Duniya ki bandish se riston ki doori se
Dharam mayne rakhta hai
Insanon ke usool bematlab ho jaate hai
Logon k fitoot mayne nhi rakhte hai magar un sabse zyada
Dharam mayne rakhta hai
Insaas ka koi auchit nahin hai
Bhagwaan ka koi astitva nahi hai magar
Dharti pr dharam mayne rakhta hai
Sikhaya hai bachpan se hume
Pyaar kro hare k dharam se par
pyaar mein pado bas apne dharam se kyuki pure
sampradaay ko sirf aur sirf
dharam mayne rakhta hai…

Diwan Shah

BIRTH PLACE : Riyadh Saudi Arabia
I am a sufi writer.

Tere hotho ki gawahi kuch aur keh rahi hai,
Teri hotho ki rasai kuch aur keh rahi hai,

Tamaseen hai yeh duniya aur tamasha bana hum mai,
Ter dastaan e mohabat kuch aur keh rahi hai,

Mere khoon ke aasu sanam tumhe nazar nahi aaye,
Tere chehre e rangat kuch aur keh rahi hai,

Mujhe bheed me bula kr ye pyaar tera jatana
Teri tanhai ki mohabat kuch aur keh rahi hai,

Tere gesu hai bkhare teri kajal kuch dhul hai,
Tere sir ki ye shikan kuch aur keh rah hai,

Tere jubaan ka ladkhadana tu bechain lag rahi hai,
Tere dl me chupi baatein kuch aur keh rahi hai,

Tu khush nahi hai jaana mere bargaah me aakr
Tere nagmo ki gawahi kuch aur keh rahi hai

Meri khwaish e duwa ha tujhe mile saja-e-gam
Pr mehboob ki mohabat kuch aur keh rahi hai.

Nikhil K

NEOWISER

The Road Of Destiny
Life Or Love

It is a road.
It won't be a straight road forever.
It twists and turns unexpectedly
Sometimes hilly
Sometimes steep
Sometimes harsh
Sometimes very soft
Sometimes you ll love the journey
Sometimes you ll hate it to the core.
At some pont you will feel like
You cannot travel anymore.
If you wish to
You can change the route.
But you ll never know
What that new road has got to offer you.

<u>Mother's Love</u>

A mother is the greatest lover.
The best healer of all the pain and fear.
A teacher who makes you so better.
A giver who always keeps you happier.
A fighter who makes you humbler.
Remember she is an achiever
.So live right for her forever.

There is no enemy
As worse as your ego
There's no friend
As good as your humbleness.

Flairs and Glairs, a platform by a student for the students. We are esteemed youth struggling to carve out our path for our future and we follow a basic mindset Since everyone is not born with all-round skills. Joining hands with people who are born to execute it with perfection is the best way to evolve. Self-Evolution is the need of the hour but, evolving as a community is what we strive for. The initiative as kickstarted by, Founder- Mr. Shubham Shah with the motive to utilize the skillset and talent of writing has now a team of 10+ people who are actively participating into newer forms of learning and discovering talents among youngsters. We Provide platform and services like Publishing opportunities, Open mics, Workshops, Hands-on training. Operating with Brand Name of Flairs and Glairs (Publication House), we offer the chance of elevating a passionate writer to an esteemed author With Brand name Teekhe Zasbaaat. We bring to you an opportunity to get accustomed with the Public Speaking and Presenting of Thoughts along with regular challenges to brush up your inking spirit. The newest initiative to extend our services we introduced in a new writing Platform- The Glittering Fables and Ink Over Tears.

We Choose to Fly Like A Falcon than to be

a Leg Pulling Crab.

To Know More: Infoline – 7781900870
Mail Us At-
flairsandglairs@gmail.com / info@flairsandglairs.in
Or Visit is at
www.flairsandglairs.com / www.flairsandglairs.in
Social Handles- @flairsandglairs @teekhezasbaaat